A TALE OF A BOY CALLED CALVIN

By

Diana Tello

Acknowledgment

"I would like to acknowledge my husband for always supporting me in every crazy thing I've wanted to do, and my children for shaping me into who I am today and being the driving force in this journey. This book, however, is something I want my grandchildren to enjoy. I want them to know that no matter how old you are, you can dream and bring those dreams to life. My grandchildren are my joy."
Always and forever.

Contents

Calvin's Dream Chronicles 1

Water World

Welcome to My World

Hi there! My name is Calvin, and I'm 10 years old. Most stories start with "Once upon a time," but my story is a bit different, and I think you're going to like it.

You see, I don't just live in the real world—I have my own worlds, full of amazing adventures where anything is possible. I love to draw, listen to music, play in the park, and swim, but what I love most is creating dreams. My imagination is like a magic key that opens doors to incredible places, and now, I want to take you with me to explore some of these worlds.

In the real world, I live with my mom, dad, sister, and two brothers. My sister, Emily, is 11, and my twin brothers, Max and Leo, are five. Our house is always noisy—Emily practicing her violin, Max and Leo running around and yelling, and my parents trying to keep everything under control. Sometimes, it feels like there's never a quiet moment.

Don't get me wrong, I love my family, but with everyone always around, it can get annoying. There are days when I just want to find a quiet corner, but it's hard when there's always something going on—a game, music, or just the usual chaos. That's when I escape to my own worlds.

You might wonder why I like living in my own world so much. Well, sometimes the real world feels too loud and busy, like there's too much happening all at once, and it makes me feel like I just need some space. So, I started creating my own worlds—places where I can be myself, where everything is calm, and where there's always something fun to do.

In my worlds, I can be anything I want, go anywhere, and do whatever I like. The best part? I'm never alone. In these worlds, being around people doesn't bother me at all. Instead, I actually enjoy it because everyone is part of the adventure, and we all get along. I have friends in every world who join me on these adventures, making each journey even more exciting.

Are you ready? Let's dive into my imagination and discover the wonders that await. Who knows? You might even find your own magical world!

CHAPTER 2

Water World

One night, as I drifted into sleep, I found myself in the most amazing underwater world—a place where the usual rules didn't seem to matter anymore. I was deep beneath the waves, but somehow, I could breathe easily, like the water was welcoming me in. This place was completely different from anything I had ever seen before. The ocean seemed to stretch out forever, glowing with the bright colors of a living coral reef, filled with all kinds of sea life.

In this world, I wasn't just floating around; I could swim as fast and smoothly as a dolphin, gliding alongside them as they leaped and played in the crystal-clear water. Every sea creature was my friend—from the giant whales that sang deep, haunting songs to the tiny, colorful fish that zipped through the water like living rainbows. The sea was alive with colors and sounds, all moving together in a perfect, beautiful dance.

We explored every hidden corner of this underwater paradise together, swimming through coral reefs that sparkled like jewels in the soft, dappled light from above. We discovered underwater caves full of secrets, with walls covered in mysterious markings and glowing crystals that lit up the space with an eerie, magical light. Each new discovery made my heart race with excitement, like I could feel the thrill of it pulsing through the water.

But it wasn't just the animals that made this world special. Deep down in the ocean, mermaids swam gracefully beside us, their shimmering tails leaving trails of light in the water. These mythical beings, who I had only imagined before, were now my friends, guiding me through the mysteries of their underwater kingdom. Their laughter sounded like music in the water, and their eyes sparkled with the knowledge of ancient secrets.

This wasn't just any dream; this was Water World—my very first true creation. Here, I wasn't just watching, I was the one making this world, shaping it with every thought, every breath. The mermaids, with their beauty and mystery, weren't just fantasy; they were exactly what I wanted in this world—peace, harmony, and a place where the noise and chaos of the real world couldn't reach me.

In Water World, I had built a kingdom under the waves where the problems of the surface couldn't touch me. Here, I could swim freely, breathe easily, and let my imagination soar through the depths of the ocean. It was a world I made myself, a sanctuary where reality and fantasy mixed, and where I could find the calm and happiness that I sometimes couldn't find when I was awake.

This was Water World—my first dream creation, a place where I could truly be free.

Meeting Krisa

One day, while exploring my underwater world, something amazing happened. I was swimming through the colorful coral, surrounded by bright fish and shimmering light, when I saw a figure coming toward me. At first, I couldn't tell what it was, but as it got closer, I saw that it was unlike anything I had ever seen before.

The creature was golden, and as the sunlight shone through the water, it sparkled with all the colors of the rainbow. It looked like a girl, but there was something magical about her. She had long, flowing hair that floated around her like silk, and her eyes were a beautiful shade of turquoise blue that seemed to hold the secrets of the ocean.

When she spoke, her voice was soft and sweet, like a gentle breeze. "My name is Krisa," she said with a kind smile. My heart started beating faster with excitement and curiosity. I had never met anyone like her before, and I felt a tingling sensation of anticipation. Her gaze was warm and friendly, making me feel safe, even though we were in the middle of a mysterious ocean.

Krisa was both strange and beautiful. Her skin glowed brightly, and her arms and legs were long and graceful. She reached out to me with her slender fingers, and though her touch was cool, it was comforting. We didn't need to talk much—it felt like we understood each other without words.

"Would you like to see where I live?" she asked, her voice full of excitement. I nodded eagerly, ready to learn more about this incredible world and the fascinating creature who lived here. Krisa gently took my hand, and together, we swam through the vibrant underwater world.

The Underwater City

As we swam through the clear blue waters, I was amazed by the beauty all around us. The coral reefs stretched out like giant underwater gardens, filled with bright colors and teeming with life. Each reef was a masterpiece, with corals of every shape and color swaying in the current. Schools of fish darted in and out of the coral, their shiny scales reflecting the light like little jewels.

Every creature seemed to belong to a different world, but they all lived together in harmony. The ocean was like a symphony, with every movement adding to the music of this underwater paradise. I felt a deep sense of peace here, like the ocean was hugging me and welcoming me into its depths.

But the most exciting discovery of all was the mermaids. They were real in this dream world, swimming gracefully among the other sea creatures. Their long, flowing hair streamed behind them like golden rivers, and they moved so smoothly, it looked like they were dancing through the water. Their tails left trails of glowing light and seeing them up close made me feel like I had stepped into one of my wildest dreams.

As we swam around the coral reefs, I felt a burst of joy and awe. The bright colors, the graceful sea creatures, and the gentle rhythm of the ocean all came together to create a scene of unmatched beauty. Every new sight made me feel thrilled, and I couldn't stop smiling. It was like I had finally found a place where I truly belonged—a world where my imagination could run free, where the noise and chaos of reality couldn't reach me.

After what felt like hours of exploring this magical underwater world, we arrived at a city like none I had ever seen. The buildings were made from giant shells, each one a work of art. Some shells shined with every color of the rainbow, while others were decorated with pearls and treasures from the sea, making the city look magical and otherworldly. The streets were busy with activity, but there was a peaceful, calm energy in the air, so different from the noisy, busy world I was used to.

Krisa led me through the winding streets, introducing me to the underwater community. Everywhere we went, people smiled warmly and greeted us with curious looks. The residents of the city were all different, each one unique, but they all shared the same welcoming spirit. The houses, which looked like giant oyster shells, were painted in colors I had never seen before, colors that seemed to change with the light.

We finally arrived at one of the houses, and Krisa told me it was her home. It was cozy and inviting, filled with treasures she had collected from her adventures under the sea. Her room was amazing, with walls covered in shimmering pearls and glowing seaweed. She showed me a costume she had—it was silver with spikes around the mask and orange accents on the arms and legs. It looked like something from another world, and I could see how proud she was as she showed it to me.

Krisa told me stories about her family, her parents who were visiting her grandparents, and her three older brothers who were full of fun and mischief. As she spoke, I felt a deep connection to this place and to Krisa. This underwater city, with its beauty, calm, and sense of community, felt like a second home to me.

In that moment, I knew that this world, this dream, was something truly special. It was a place where I could escape, be free, and let my imagination soar without limits. And with Krisa by my side, I knew that the adventures here were only just beginning.

CHAPTER 5

The Adventures Begin

Each night, as the world above went dark, I couldn't wait to return to my dreams, my special place. Krisa was always there, a constant friend as we went on countless adventures beneath the waves. We explored dazzling coral reefs that looked like underwater gardens, their bright colors making everything look magical. Together, we swam through mysterious underwater caves filled with secrets and treasures waiting to be found. We played with the friendly sea creatures that lived in this world—gentle dolphins, playful sea turtles, and even the occasional mermaid who would join us in our games, her laughter echoing through the water.

But one night, when I drifted into sleep, something felt different. The bright colors of the coral were not as bright, and there was a strange feeling in the water. The calm currents that usually swayed the seaweed were now wild, churning with an unsettling energy. A deep rumble echoed through the sea, shaking me to the core like a distant growl from a huge creature. I looked around, my heart beating faster as a sense of unease settled in.

The usually friendly sea creatures were now swimming in all directions, their movements frantic and confused. Schools of fish scattered like tiny shards of glass, and even the playful dolphins were nowhere to be seen. The water, which had always been clear and welcoming, had turned dark, swirling with powerful currents that kicked up sand and debris, making it hard to see and adding to my growing worry.

Krisa appeared by my side; her face serious as she looked around. "Something's wrong," she said, her voice full of worry. I could see it too—the signs were everywhere. The sea was no longer the safe, magical place it had always been. Something was coming, something powerful and dangerous.

A great underwater storm was brewing, one like the sea world had never seen before.

CHAPTER 6

The Storm

The storm hit with a sudden, terrifying force, like the ocean itself had turned against us. The once peaceful underwater world became a wild, raging storm, stronger than anything I had ever seen. The calm waves turned into giant, crashing walls of water, and the currents that used to be soft and inviting were now pulling at me with all their might. Fear gripped me so tightly that I could barely move. The water, usually so clear and blue, was now dark and angry, and it felt like the ocean was trying to pull me away from the world I had come to love. My heart raced, my mind filled with panic and confusion.

But even in the middle of all that fear, a spark of determination grew inside me, pushing back against the storm. This world had become my second home, a place where I had made friends and had amazing adventures, and I couldn't let it be destroyed. The thought of losing everything—Krisa, my new friends, the beauty of this underwater world—filled me with a fire that burned away my fear. I couldn't let the storm win; I wouldn't.

I looked to Krisa, my friend and guide in this strange and wonderful world. Her turquoise eyes, usually so calm and friendly, now mirrored the wild energy of the storm. But even though she was scared, I could see a strength in her that reminded me why I had trusted her from the start. "We have to act quickly," she said, her voice steady and firm despite the chaos all around us. She was like the calm center of the storm, and her bravery gave me the courage I needed to face what was coming.

I nodded, feeling the fear mix with a newfound bravery. The responsibility on my shoulders was heavy, almost too much to bear, but it didn't stop me. Instead, it pushed me forward, driving me to action. I realized then that this wasn't just a dream, not just an adventure—it was a test, a challenge that would shape who I was and who I would become. I couldn't fail—not when so much was at risk.

Krisa's hand found mine, her grip firm and comforting. "We'll get through this," she promised, her voice a beacon of hope in the storm. The cool warmth of her touch grounded me, giving me the strength to focus on what needed to be done. Together, we would face this challenge, and together, we would protect the world we had come to love. The bond we shared was unbreakable, built on the adventures and challenges we had already faced, and I knew that no storm could tear us apart.

As we dived into the heart of the storm, the once clear and bright water now churned with darkness and debris. But I was no longer the scared boy who had first stumbled into this underwater world. I was a protector, a guardian of a world that had given me so much. And I would fight for it with everything I had. The storm might rage around us, but it would never defeat our determination.

CHAPTER 7

The Battle to Save the City

The storm raged on, the water churning wildly, and the once-strong shell houses of the sea people were now in danger of being washed away. The marine creatures, usually so graceful and calm, were caught in the storm's fury, struggling to stay together. My heart pounded as I saw the fear in their eyes, and I knew they were counting on Krisa and me.

Krisa took the lead, rallying the sea people with a determination that filled me with hope. Her voice rang out, clear and strong, as she guided them to safer areas and helped them work together. The sea people, trusting Krisa's leadership, began to strengthen their homes and protect the younger and smaller creatures from the storm.

Meanwhile, my mind raced with ideas. I remembered the ocean books I had read, filled with information about tides, currents, and marine life. We needed to calm the storm's force and redirect its energy away from the shell city. But how?

Then, an idea hit me—a spark of inspiration in the middle of the chaos. If we could channel the storm's energy into a controlled path, we might be able to protect the city. But we needed something strong enough to withstand the storm's force while guiding it away from the fragile shell houses.

"Krisa," I shouted over the roaring storm, "we need to build a barrier, something that can direct the storm's energy away from the city!"

Her eyes lit up with understanding. "The Great Reef!" she exclaimed; her voice full of hope. "It's strong and big enough to act as a natural barrier. If we can reinforce it and redirect the current, we might be able to save the city."

Without wasting any time, we swam toward the Great Reef, the heart of the underwater world. The storm made it almost impossible to move, but we pushed forward, driven by the lives of our friends and the fate of the city. As we reached the reef, we saw that it was already being battered by the storm. Pieces of coral were breaking off, the sea life that usually thrived there had scattered, and the once-strong reef was starting to weaken.

"We need to act fast!" Krisa called out; her voice barely heard over the howling currents. "We have to reinforce the reef and create a path to guide the storm's energy away from the city."

Using our knowledge and the resources around us, we began to work with a speed that left no room for mistakes. Krisa, with her quick hands and smart thinking, gathered strong seaweed and vines, weaving them into a net-like structure to hold the reef together. Meanwhile, I focused on imagining a design that could channel the storm's energy without breaking under the pressure.

As we worked, the sea people joined us, their fear turning into determination. Dolphins used their strength to push large rocks into place, creating a foundation for our barrier. Mermaids, with their skilled hands, helped secure the netting, weaving it through the coral and anchoring it with shells and stones. Even the smallest sea creatures played their part, offering anything they could find to help strengthen the barrier that would protect their home.

The storm kept raging, but slowly, our barrier started to take shape. The netting, reinforced by rocks and shells, began to hold, and we could see the effect it was having—the current started to shift, the storm's energy being directed away from the city and into the open ocean where it couldn't cause any harm. Seeing this gave us hope, knowing that our efforts were making a difference.

But the battle wasn't over yet. The storm, as if sensing our resistance, unleashed one final, massive wave—a wave so huge that it threatened to destroy everything we had built. My heart pounded as I realized that if this wave hit, it could destroy not just the barrier but the entire city we had fought so hard to protect.

"We need to hold the barrier!" Krisa shouted, her voice filled with urgency and determination. "Everyone, push with all your strength!"

In that moment, it felt like time slowed down. The roar of the water was deafening, the weight of the wave pressing down on us with unimaginable force. Every muscle in my body strained against the pressure, the effort of holding the barrier pushing me to the edge of my strength. But I wasn't alone—Krisa, the sea people, the dolphins, the mermaids, and even the smallest sea creatures—all of us stood together, united in our determination to save the city.

Just when it seemed like we couldn't hold on any longer, something incredible happened. The wave, once so powerful and unstoppable, began to lose its strength. The barrier we had built held firm, and with one final, desperate push, we redirected the wave away from the city, watching as it crashed harmlessly into the open ocean. A sigh of relief echoed through the water as the storm, finally spent, began to calm down. The wild currents softened into gentle waves, and the once-chaotic sea returned to its peaceful state.

A New Beginning

As the storm finally passed, the underwater world began to feel hopeful. The once wild waters calmed, and the sea creatures slowly emerged from their hiding places. The ocean, which had been a battlefield just moments ago, now shimmered with a peaceful calm. The shell city, though battered, stood strong—a symbol of teamwork, resilience, and the unbreakable spirit of its inhabitants.

Krisa and I shared a look of relief and accomplishment. We had faced the storm's fury and won, protecting the city and the friends we had come to care about deeply. It was a moment that felt almost unreal, as if time had slowed down to let us fully appreciate what we had done. I knew this was a memory that would stay with me forever—a reminder of what we could achieve when we worked together.

"Thank you, Calvin," Krisa said softly, her voice filled with gratitude. "Without you, we wouldn't have made it."

I smiled back at her, feeling a warm glow in my chest. "I couldn't have done it without you, Krisa. This world is as much yours as it is mine."

As we spoke, the sea people gathered around us, their faces glowing with admiration and thanks. Their eyes sparkled with joy and relief, and they brought us gifts from the ocean—shiny pearls, intricate shells, and treasures that gleamed like stars. But as I accepted their gifts, I knew that the greatest treasure wasn't something I could hold in my hands. It was the bond we had formed, a connection that brought us together in a way I had never known before. We were no longer just inhabitants of the same world; we were a family, united by the challenges we had faced and the victory we had won.

As we swam back to the city, a deep sense of peace washed over me. The underwater world, once threatened by the storm, had become a place of safety and joy again. The once-dark waters now glistened with new life, and the city, though scarred, stood proudly against the vast ocean. And I realized something important—this world, born from my imagination, was more than just a dream. It was a place where I could always return, to explore, to play, and to dream without limits.

"Krisa," I said, turning to her, "there was a moment during the storm when I thought I couldn't do it. I was so scared that I wanted to give in to the fear." I paused, remembering how strong that fear had been, then continued, "But when I thought about you, the city, all our friends, I found something inside me. Even though I was afraid, I found the courage to keep going."

Krisa looked at me, her eyes shining with understanding. "That's what being brave means, Calvin. It's not about never being scared; it's about moving forward even when you are. And you did it because you care about others. That's true courage."

With a gentle smile, she reached into a small pouch she carried and pulled out a shell, delicate and sparkling. "This is for you," she said softly, placing it in my hand. "Whenever you look at this shell, remember that this world and our friendship will always be a part of you."

Her words resonated in my heart. I had learned something important: that fear wasn't something to be ashamed of, but something I could overcome when I cared enough. I knew I could always find that courage within me, and that lesson was as valuable as any other treasure I had found in my adventures.

That night, as I drifted into sleep, I felt a calmness in my heart. I had faced my fears and emerged stronger. Courage didn't mean not being afraid; it meant acting despite the fear, and now I knew I could always be brave when it mattered. With that reassurance, I let myself slip into the world of dreams, knowing I was ready for whatever adventure came next, hoping that each new journey would bring a new and better world into my life.

I knew my journey was far from over. There were countless worlds waiting to be discovered, endless adventures yet to be had, new friends to meet, and new lessons to learn. The underwater world with Krisa was just the beginning—the first of many dream creations that lay ahead. The thought filled me with excitement and anticipation, reminding me that my imagination held endless possibilities.

And with that comforting thought, I closed my eyes, ready to dream once more.

The shell was smooth and cool in my hand, its colors shifting in the light like the waters of the sea. As I held it, I felt a sense of calm and reassurance. The dream world might fade, but this shell was real—a memory of my adventures and the courage I discovered, something I could hold onto even when I was awake.

As the dream began to dissolve, the bright colors of the underwater world softened into the gentle darkness of sleep. My grip tightened around the shell, and with one last look at Krisa, I whispered, "I'll never forget."

And then, with a final, peaceful sigh, the dream ended.

I woke up in my room, the early morning light softly filling the space. For a moment, I lay still, the images of the dream fresh in my mind. Then, as I sat up, I felt something in my hand. There, resting in my palm, was the shell—smooth, cool, and very real. A wide smile spread across my face as I realized that the magical world I had just left wasn't truly gone. It was with me forever.

The shell was a comforting reminder that the world of my dreams wasn't just in my imagination, but a real place where I could return whenever I closed my eyes. And with that thought, I felt a deep sense of peace and joy. I knew that this was just the beginning of many more adventures to come.

IS THIS THE END OR THE BEGINNING?

This feels like the beginning of something extraordinary. The adventures I embark on are just the start of my journey through the worlds I create. With each new dream, I open the door to endless possibilities, friendships, and discoveries. So, while one adventure may end, it's just paving the way for the next. In my world, there's always more to explore, more to imagine, and more to dream.

So, no—this is far from the end.

CHAPTER 9

A New World Awaits

The next time I closed my eyes, I found myself in a completely different place. Gone were the shimmering waters and coral reefs; instead, I was surrounded by towering trees, their leaves whispering secrets in the breeze. The air was filled with the scent of pine and wildflowers, and the ground beneath my feet was soft with moss.

I was in a magical forest, a place where every tree had a story, and every creature could speak. The light filtering through the branches was golden, casting a warm glow over everything. As I took in the beauty of this new world, I felt a sense of excitement bubbling up inside me.

"Welcome to the Magical Forest," a voice said from behind me.

I turned to see a wise old owl perched on a low branch, his large, amber eyes watching me with a knowing expression. His feathers were a mix of browns and grays, giving him a look of age and wisdom. "I've been expecting you, Calvin," he said with a nod.

"Who are you?" I asked, curious.

"I'm Ollivander, the guardian of this forest," the owl replied, his voice deep and calm. "This is a place of magic and mystery, where the trees hold secrets, and the animals are more than they seem. And you, Calvin, have been chosen to go on a quest that will take you to the heart of this forest, to a place where a great treasure is hidden."

"A treasure?" I asked, my eyes wide with wonder.

Ollivander nodded. "Yes, a treasure with the power to heal, to bring peace and joy to all who find it. But it won't be an easy journey. You'll face challenges, solve riddles, and make choices that will test your courage and kindness."

I felt a thrill of excitement and a bit of nervousness. "I'm ready," I said, feeling determined.

Ollivander smiled, a twinkle in his eyes. "Then let the adventure begin."

With that, the wise old owl flew up into the sky, leading me deeper into the Magical Forest, where new friends, challenges, and magical experiences awaited. I knew this was just the beginning of another incredible dream world, a place where anything was possible and where my imagination could soar.

The Next Adventure: The enchanted Forest

To be continued…

Calvin's Dream Chronicles 2

The Enchanted Garden

The Living Garden

Calvin and Krisa stepped through the portal and into a garden that looked like something out of a dream. They stood at the entrance of a magical place, bigger than any garden they had ever seen before. The air around them was warm, carrying the sweet smell of flowers and the soft sound of leaves rustling in the breeze. Above, the sky was bright blue with puffy clouds floating by slowly. But what really made them stop and stare wasn't just how beautiful the garden was—it was how alive everything seemed.

Everywhere they looked, the garden wasn't just full of life; it was full of magic. The flowers, bursting with color, turned their heads to follow Calvin and Krisa as they walked. It was like the flowers were watching them, and their petals fluttered like tiny eyelashes blinking at them. The tall trees, strong and graceful, seemed to sway as if they were dancing to music only they could hear. Their branches leaned down, offering shade and whispering softly, like they had secrets to share. Even the grass under their feet felt different, as if it was humming with a gentle, soothing energy that flowed through the earth.

Calvin looked at Krisa, both of their eyes wide with wonder. "This isn't just any garden," Calvin said in awe. "It's alive!"

Krisa nodded, amazed. "It feels like a dream, but it's real!"

As they wandered deeper into the garden, a wise old owl swooped down from the trees, his feathers a mix of browns and golds. "Welcome, young traveler," the owl hooted, his eyes gleaming with wisdom. "I am Orin, guardian of the knowledge of this land."

Calvin smiled, excited to meet such a majestic creature. "Hello, Orin."

Before Orin could speak further, a playful fox darted out from behind a bush. His red fur shimmered in the sunlight as he grinned at Calvin. "I'm Finn! I've heard all about you! Are you ready for some fun adventures?"

Calvin laughed at Finn's mischievous grin, but before he could respond, a soft glow filled the clearing. Emerging gracefully from the trees was a majestic unicorn with a shimmering silver coat and a long, flowing mane that sparkled like stardust. Her eyes sparkled with kindness and wisdom, and she radiated a calming, magical energy.

"I am Seraphina," the unicorn said in a voice as soothing as a gentle breeze. "I have been waiting for you. There is something special we need to show you."

Calvin was filled with awe. "What is it?"

"We are on a quest," Orin explained. "There is a hidden waterfall deep within this garden, and its waters have magical healing powers. But the path to it is filled with challenges and riddles."

Finn bounded forward, his tail wagging. "And that's where the fun comes in! Together, we can find it!"

Seraphina stepped forward; her soft voice filled with calm encouragement. "The garden has many wonders, but it also holds dangers. Darkness seeks to destroy what is beautiful here. Only by working together and using our wisdom and courage can we succeed."

Calvin felt his heart race with excitement and purpose. "We'll do it," he said, turning to Krisa. "We'll help them find the waterfall and protect the garden."

Krisa smiled, feeling the same sense of adventure. "Yes, let's go."

And so, with Orin the wise owl, Finn the playful fox, and Seraphina the majestic unicorn as their guides, Calvin and Krisa set off deeper into the Enchanted Garden. They knew the journey ahead would test their courage and strength, but they were ready. Together, they would face whatever challenges awaited them, knowing that the magic of the garden would guide them on their quest.

CHAPTER 2

The Whispering Willows

Calvin, Krisa, Orin, Finn, and Seraphina continued deeper into the Enchanted Garden, following the winding path that twisted like a snake through the thick foliage. Each step felt more magical, and their bond grew stronger with every challenge they faced together. Soon, the trees around them changed, and they found themselves in a grove filled with towering willows. These willows weren't like the other trees they had seen before. Their long, delicate branches drooped down like curtains of green silk, swaying gently in the wind.

But what made these willows truly special was the sound they made. As the wind moved through their leaves, it sounded like they were whispering to one another, sharing secrets that only they could understand.

"Do you hear that?" Calvin asked, his eyes wide with curiosity.

Krisa nodded; her gaze fixed on the trees. "It's like they're...talking."

Orin, perched on a low branch nearby, tilted his head. "These are the Whispering Willows, guardians of ancient knowledge. They hold many secrets, but only those with true wisdom can understand them."

Finn bounced on his paws, his tail wagging with excitement. "Sounds like a challenge! Let's figure it out!"

Seraphina, her silver coat shimmering in the soft light, stepped forward gracefully. "We must listen carefully. The willows will test us, but with patience and harmony, we can find the answers."

As they stepped closer, the whispering grew louder. The branches of the willows seemed to lean toward them, eager to share their knowledge.

"Welcome, young ones," the willows whispered in unison. Their voices were soft but powerful, filling the air like a gentle breeze. "We are the Whispering Willows, guardians of ancient knowledge. To move forward, you must prove your wisdom."

Calvin and Krisa exchanged glances. They had been expecting challenges, but this was different. These trees didn't want to test their strength or bravery—they wanted to test their minds.

"What must we do?" Krisa asked, stepping forward confidently.

The willows swayed gracefully, their branches brushing together like the pages of a giant book. "You must solve a riddle," they said. "It is an old riddle, passed down through the ages. Only those with true wisdom can solve it. If you succeed, the way forward will be revealed."

Orin's wise eyes gleamed as he hooted softly. "Riddles often require you to think beyond what you see. Trust in your instincts."

The willows' leaves rustled, and their voices blended into one. "Here is your riddle: I speak without a mouth, and I hear without ears. I have no body, but I come alive with the wind. What am I?"

Calvin furrowed his brow, thinking hard. The riddle was tricky, but the answer was there, just out of reach. He could feel it.

Krisa closed her eyes, repeating the riddle in her head. "I speak without a mouth... I hear without ears..." she murmured.

Finn twitched his ears, his excitement bubbling over. "Oh, come on, I love riddles! What could it be?"

Seraphina's soothing voice calmed the group. "Listen not just with your ears but with your heart. The garden's magic will guide you."

Inspired by her words, Calvin tilted his head and listened closely. As the wind moved through the willow branches, he realized something.

"It's an echo!" Calvin said confidently, his eyes lighting up.

The willows' leaves trembled with joy, their whispers growing brighter and lighter. "You have answered wisely," they said. "The path forward is now open to you. But remember, wisdom is not just about knowing the right answers—it's about understanding the world around you and listening to those who came before."

Orin hooted approvingly. "An answer found by listening closely—very wise indeed."

Finn jumped up, wagging his tail in delight. "I knew you'd get it, Calvin!"

Seraphina nodded with a serene smile. "The magic of the garden grows stronger in us all."

As the willows' branches parted, revealing a glowing path ahead, Calvin and Krisa felt a renewed sense of determination. The garden was depending on them, and with their friends by their side, they knew they wouldn't let it down.

Together, they stepped onto the glowing path, ready for whatever came next.

CHAPTER 3

The Song of the Streams

Calvin, Krisa, Orin, Finn, and Seraphina followed the glowing path that twisted and turned through the Enchanted Garden. The further they walked, the more the air filled with a soft, magical energy. Eventually, they arrived at a peaceful stream that looked like a shiny ribbon of silver weaving through the garden. The water sparkled in the sunlight, reflecting the sky above, and seemed to dance with colors. As they approached, a gentle melody filled the air, like a lullaby sung by the earth itself.

The stream wasn't just a stream—it was alive, just like everything else in the garden. Its gentle waves moved in time with the music, as if the water itself was singing. Calvin and Krisa knelt down by the water's edge, listening closely to the beautiful song that filled the air.

"Wow, it's like the water is making music," Krisa whispered, her eyes wide with wonder.

Seraphina stepped forward, her silver mane shimmering in the sunlight. "This is no ordinary stream. The Song of the Streams flows through it, keeping the garden alive and in balance."

"Balance is key," Orin added wisely, his feathers ruffling in the breeze. "The stream's song is the very heartbeat of the garden."

Just then, the water's melody became clearer, and a sweet, melodic voice sang out from the stream itself. "Welcome, travelers," it said, its tone as smooth and flowing as the water. "I am the Song of the Streams, the melody that keeps the garden in harmony. If you wish to continue your journey, you must first understand the music of the world."

Finn's ears perked up. "Music of the world? That sounds fun!" he said, wagging his tail.

Krisa gazed into the stream, her reflection mingling with the ripples. "But how do we understand the music?" she asked, her voice full of curiosity.

The stream's voice was gentle and wise. "The world is filled with music, even if you can't always hear it right away. Each sound is a note in the song of life. The rustle of the leaves, the chirping of birds, the wind in the trees—they are all part of this song. To pass this trial, you must listen carefully and create your own song that reflects the harmony of the garden."

Seraphina's horn glowed softly. "Close your eyes and listen with more than your ears. The garden will guide you."

Orin nodded in agreement. "Understanding goes beyond what you hear—it's about feeling the rhythm of life itself."

Calvin and Krisa looked at each other, realizing this challenge would take more than just listening. They had to connect with the garden's magic in their hearts. Closing their eyes, they focused on the sounds around them: the rustling leaves, the chirping birds, the gentle whispers of the wind as it moved through the branches.

Finn stood quietly, his ears twitching as he listened to the music of the world, while Seraphina radiated calm energy, helping the group stay focused.

Calvin took a deep breath and began to hum, his voice low and steady like the gentle flow of the stream. The tune came from deep within him, as though the garden itself was singing through him. Krisa listened for a moment before joining in, her voice light and airy like the wind, weaving through Calvin's melody. Together, they created a song that echoed the sounds of the garden—the rhythm of the leaves, the melody of the birds, the hum of the earth.

Orin's hoots and Finn's playful yips blended into the song, while Seraphina's presence added a quiet, harmonious hum to complete the melody.

As they sang, the stream began to glow with a soft, golden light. Its water shimmered, and the song of the stream merged with their voices, creating a perfect harmony. It was as if the entire garden was singing with them.

"You have done well," the stream's voice sang, filled with joy and approval. "Your song shows that you understand the magic and harmony of the garden. The melody of life flows through you now, guiding your every step."

The water in the stream started to move more quickly, form-ing a clear path deeper into the garden. Calvin and his friends smiled at each other, feeling proud of what they had accom-plished. The song they had created brought them closer to the magic of the garden, and now the stream itself was leading them forward.

"Onward!" Finn barked happily, bouncing ahead.

Orin fluttered his wings. "We have learned the power of harmony. Let's carry it with us."

Seraphina's eyes sparkled. "The garden's magic grows strong-er within each of you. You are ready for whatever comes next."

They stood up and followed the path created by the flowing water, their spirits lifted by the music that still echoed in their hearts. The garden's harmony had become a part of them, and they knew that whatever challenges lay ahead, they would face them together.

CHAPTER 4

The Guardians of the Grove

Calvin, Krisa, Orin, Finn, and Seraphina followed the path created by the flowing stream, feeling more connected to the garden with every step they took. The air was cool and fresh, filled with the scent of pine trees and blooming flowers. As the path twisted and turned, leading them to a new part of the garden, the sense of magic seemed to deepen, filling the air around them with an otherworldly energy.

They found themselves standing at the edge of a quiet grove. Tall trees surrounded them, their thick trunks stretching high into the sky. The branches overhead formed a canopy of green, and the sunlight filtered through the leaves, casting a soft glow over everything. It was peaceful, but Calvin could sense something important waiting for them here, as if the very trees held ancient secrets.

Suddenly, the ground beneath their feet trembled, and a deep, rumbling voice echoed through the grove.

"Welcome, young travelers," the voice said. It seemed to come from the trees themselves, as if the very earth was speaking to them. "We are the Guardians of the Grove, protectors of this sacred place. You have passed the trials of the Whispering Willows and the Song of the Streams, but your journey is far from over."

Orin's feathers ruffled slightly as he nodded. "The guardians are ancient. They've been here since the garden was first created."

Krisa looked around, her eyes wide with wonder. "Who are you?" she asked, her voice filled with curiosity.

A great oak tree, even larger and more majestic than the others, seemed to move slightly, its leaves rustling as if it were taking a deep breath. "We are the oldest trees in the Enchanted Garden," the oak explained. "Our roots run deep, connecting us to the magic of this land. We have stood here for centuries, watching over the garden and protecting it from harm. But now, a dark force threatens to destroy everything."

Calvin's heart raced. "What kind of dark force?" he asked, already guessing the answer.

The oak's branches shuddered. "A darkness that seeks to take over the garden, to twist and corrupt all that is good. It grows stronger each day, and soon it may break through the barriers that protect this place."

Finn crouched low, his fur bristling. "We won't let that happen. Not on our watch!"

Seraphina stepped forward, her silver mane shimmering in the dappled sunlight. "Darkness can only grow if balance is lost. The garden's magic depends on harmony—between the plants, the creatures, and the magic that flows through us all."

Krisa stepped forward, her voice steady with determination. "We're here to help. What do we need to do?"

The trees seemed to pause, as if they were considering her words. Then, the oak spoke again. "To protect the garden, you must prove yourselves worthy of its most powerful magic. But first, you must show that you understand the balance of life—the connection between all living things."

"How do we do that?" Calvin asked, glancing at his friends.

A smaller tree, with silver leaves that shimmered in the sunlight, spoke up, its branches swaying gently. "You will face three challenges," it said. "Each one will test your understanding of the garden's magic and the balance that keeps it alive. Only by passing these challenges can you unlock the power needed to stop the darkness."

Orin blinked his wise eyes slowly. "These challenges won't test your strength or speed—they'll test your heart and your understanding of the magic that binds us all."

Calvin and Krisa exchanged a glance. They had faced challenges before, but these felt different. They weren't just about physical courage—they were about wisdom, patience, and understanding the deeper magic of the garden.

"We're ready," Krisa said firmly, her voice filled with determination.

Finn bounded forward eagerly. "Bring it on!"

The great oak tree bent its branches low, forming a passage between the trees. "Then step forward," it said, "and begin the first challenge."

As Calvin, Krisa, and their friends entered the grove, the air around them seemed to shift. It was cooler now, and the ground beneath their feet felt soft and alive, as if it were pulsing with energy. The trees loomed overhead, ancient and wise, watching their every move. Calvin could feel the weight of the garden's magic pressing around them, but it wasn't overwhelming—it was inviting, asking them to trust in the journey ahead.

Seraphina's voice was calm and steady. "Remember, we are not alone. The garden's magic flows through us. Together, we will face what's to come."

The group pressed on, knowing that the challenges ahead would test everything they had learned. The fate of the Enchanted Garden rested on their shoulders, and they couldn't turn back now.

CHAPTER 5

The Final Confrontation

As the light from the garden spread through every corner, Calvin, Krisa, Orin, Finn, and Seraphina could feel the air around them change. The once peaceful atmosphere grew heavy with tension, like a storm waiting to break. The sky, which had been clear and blue, now darkened, turning into a swirling mass of angry clouds. A cold wind swept through the garden, carrying the sour scent of decay and danger. The flowers, once bright and tall, now drooped, their colors fading as if drained by the approaching darkness.

Calvin looked up at the sky and knew the final battle was near.

"They're coming," Krisa whispered, her voice calm but serious. She could sense the darkness gathering, its power growing stronger by the second.

Calvin nodded, feeling his heart race. "We've learned so much from this place, from the guardians and the garden itself. We can't let it fall now."

Krisa's eyes narrowed with determination. "We won't. The garden is counting on us, and we're not alone."

Around them, the garden's guardians gathered. The Whispering Willows rustled their leaves in a quiet but determined murmur. The streams glowed softly, the Song of the Streams filling the air with a quiet, hopeful melody. The ancient oak trees, with their deep roots and powerful branches, stood tall and firm, ready to defend their home. Animals of all kinds—deer, birds, butterflies—gathered around Calvin and Krisa, forming a protective circle. The entire garden seemed alive with a shared purpose.

Orin landed on a nearby branch, his eyes sharp and vigilant. "The darkness may be powerful, but together, we are stronger."

Finn crouched low, his fur bristling with excitement. "We've got this. No shadowy monster is taking down our garden!"

Seraphina stepped forward, her horn glowing softly as she radiated calm and strength. "Harmony will always prevail over chaos. We must hold onto that truth."

"We must stand together," Krisa said firmly. "The garden has given us its secrets, its songs, and its strength. Now, we need to use all of it."

Calvin took a deep breath and nodded, trying to keep his fear in check. "We're ready. We've solved the riddles, unlocked the garden's magic, and found its song. We can fight this."

Suddenly, the ground shook as the darkness began to take shape. At first, it was just a thick, swirling cloud, but then it became more defined—a towering figure made of pure shadow, its eyes burning like red-hot coals. Long, twisting tendrils of darkness stretched out from its form, reaching for the garden, eager to consume everything in its path. It was the embodiment of chaos and destruction, an ancient force that had waited for this moment to take over the garden and wipe out its magic forever.

The dark figure loomed closer, and the garden seemed to hold its breath.

But Calvin, Krisa, Orin, Finn, and Seraphina stood tall, at the center of the circle formed by the guardians. They weren't afraid. They had been preparing for this moment ever since they entered the Enchanted Garden. The lessons from the willows, the song of the stream, and the wisdom of the trees filled them with courage.

"Now!" Krisa said, her voice strong.

Together, Calvin and Krisa began to sing the song they had created with the stream. It was a melody filled with life, hope, and the harmony of the garden. Orin's wise hoots blended in, while Finn's playful yips added energy to the tune. Seraphina's voice, soft and steady, wrapped around the melody like a gentle breeze.

As their voices rose into the air, the garden responded. The trees swayed to the rhythm, their leaves shimmering with light. The streams glowed brighter, and even the flowers, though weakened, lifted their heads. The song spread through the air like a ripple, touching every corner of the garden.

The darkness hissed, recoiling as the melody reached it. The burning red eyes flickered, and the tendrils of shadow pulled back slightly, as if the dark force was struggling to keep its form.

But Calvin and Krisa didn't stop. They sang louder, their voices blending with the song of the streams and the whispers of the willows. Orin, Finn, and Seraphina joined in, their voices strengthening the song. The garden's light grew stronger, pushing against the darkness. It wasn't just a battle of magic—it was a battle of will, of harmony versus chaos.

The dark figure roared, its voice like thunder, shaking the ground. The tendrils lashed out, trying to reach Calvin and Krisa, but they were protected by the circle of guardians. The light from the garden held strong, pushing the darkness back.

"We have to finish this," Calvin said, his voice barely above a whisper but filled with determination. He knew that they had to give everything they had—every bit of strength, every ounce of hope.

Krisa nodded, her eyes locked on the shadowy figure. "Together," she said.

With one final burst of energy, Calvin, Krisa, and their friends sang the last, most powerful note of the song. The melody swelled, and the light of the garden exploded outward in a brilliant flash. The dark figure screamed, its form breaking apart into a thousand pieces. The tendrils of shadow vanished, and the burning red eyes blinked out of existence.

In a matter of moments, the darkness was gone.

The garden fell silent for a moment, as if it was taking a breath after the battle. Then, slowly, the light returned. The flowers lifted their heads, their colors bright and vibrant once again. The trees swayed gently; their branches full of life. The streams shimmered with a soft glow, and the wind carried the song of the garden through the air, as peaceful and calm as it had been before.

"We did it," Calvin said softly, almost in disbelief.

Krisa smiled, her eyes shining with relief and pride. "We did."

The garden's guardians gathered around them, their voices filled with gratitude. "You have saved the Enchanted Garden," the great oak tree said. "Your bravery, your wisdom, and your understanding of the magic within this place have restored balance. The garden will live on, thanks to you."

Orin hooted approvingly. "You've done something remarkable, young ones."

Finn grinned and wagged his tail. "We make a great team, don't we?"

Seraphina bowed her head gracefully. "The garden's harmony has been restored because of all of you. The light will always shine here."

Calvin and Krisa looked at each other, feeling a deep sense of accomplishment. They had faced the darkness and won, not just with strength, but with the magic and harmony they had learned from the garden—and from each other.

CHAPTER 6

The Garden Reborn

Calvin and Krisa sat by the stream, watching as the garden slowly came back to life after the battle. The flowers stood taller, their colors brighter, and the air seemed filled with new energy. Yet, as they rested, a small group of creatures approached—some Calvin and Krisa had met before, and others were new.

The first to arrive was the wise old tortoise with the jeweled shell. He moved slowly, but every step was deliberate. He stopped in front of them and bowed his head. "You two have done well," the tortoise said in his deep, thoughtful voice. "The garden will thrive because of your bravery and understanding."

Calvin smiled, feeling a warmth in his chest. "Thank you, but we couldn't have done it without the garden's help."

The tortoise nodded slowly. "True, but remember, the garden's magic is only as strong as those who care for it. You have shown that wisdom, like the slow steps of a journey, leads to great things."

Next, the bright butterflies fluttered around Calvin and Krisa, their wings shimmering with colors. "We carried messages across the garden," one of the butterflies said, her voice like a tinkling bell. "The garden creatures believed in you. You brought us all together, and that unity is the strongest magic."

Krisa reached out her hand, and a butterfly landed gently on her finger. "So, it wasn't just us—it was everyone working together."

The butterfly nodded. "Exactly. Harmony between all living things makes the garden strong."

As more creatures gathered—talking animals, whispering flowers, and the glowing trees—they each shared their thanks and their part in helping to save the garden.

Orin flew down from the trees and landed softly beside them. "I have seen many battles in the garden, but none like this. You've shown true wisdom in your choices," the owl said, his deep eyes gleaming with pride. "Remember, knowledge is not just about learning—it's about knowing when to act."

Finn bounded up to Calvin, wagging his tail. "You were amazing! We all were!" he said, his eyes bright with excitement. "Teamwork saved the day. And, well, a little bit of fun too!"

Seraphina approached last, her soft, glowing presence calming the air around them. "You've restored balance to the garden," she said in her gentle voice. "But remember, balance is fragile, and it must be protected. You carry that wisdom with you now, and it will serve you well beyond this place."

The great oak tree, with its deep roots and towering branches, looked down at Calvin and Krisa with pride. "We have watched you learn and grow," the oak tree said. "But remember, the greatest lesson from this adventure is not just the magic of the garden. It's the understanding that balance, patience, and working together can overcome even the darkest times."

Calvin thought about the challenges they had faced—the riddles, the song, and the final battle. It all made sense now. "So, it's not just magic," Calvin said, his voice soft. "It's about taking time to understand things, working with others, and believing that we can make a difference."

The oak tree's branches swayed, as if nodding in agreement. "Yes, and that lesson will serve you well, even outside this garden. The magic of balance, patience, and unity is not just for this world—it exists in yours too."

Calvin and Krisa stood up, feeling stronger and wiser than before. They had saved the garden, but they had also learned something valuable that they could take home with them. The creatures of the garden smiled and waved as Calvin and Krisa prepared to leave, but this wasn't a goodbye—it was more like a promise that they would always carry the magic of the garden within them.

CHAPTER 7

A New Journey Begins

As the first light of dawn filtered through the trees, Calvin and Krisa stood at the edge of the Enchanted Garden. The flowers waved gently in the breeze, and the animals and guardians watched from afar, sending them off with warm smiles.

"I'm going to miss them," Krisa said, waving at a cluster of glowing flowers that sang softly as they swayed.

Calvin nodded. "Me too, but they're right. We'll carry the magic with us, no matter where we go."

Just as they were about to take their first steps out of the garden, the silver-leafed tree they had met earlier spoke up. "Calvin, before you leave, there is something important you must remember."

Calvin turned, listening closely.

"The strength you've found here isn't just from the garden's magic. It's from inside you. Whenever you face challenges in your own world, remember what you've learned: slow down, observe, and work together. Patience and balance are just as powerful there as they are here."

Calvin smiled, feeling the truth of the words sink in. "I understand," he said. "Sometimes, when things get tough back home, I rush into them without thinking. But now I know that slowing down and looking for the bigger picture—like we did with the riddles and the song—can make all the difference."

Krisa nodded in agreement. "And just like we needed the help of the garden's creatures, we can ask for help in our world too. We don't have to face everything alone."

The silver-leafed tree shimmered. "That is the greatest lesson you can take from here. But I also have a gift for you, something that will remind you of this place."

The tree's silver leaves trembled gently, and one of the leaves broke free, floating down toward Calvin. As it touched his hand, he noticed the leaf was soft yet strong, glowing with a faint light. It felt alive, pulsing with the magic of the garden.

"This leaf is special," the silver-leafed tree said. "It holds the memory of the garden's harmony. Whenever you need to remember the lessons you've learned here, or feel lost, just hold it and listen to its song."

Calvin stared at the leaf in awe. "Thank you," he whispered. "I'll keep it with me always."

Krisa smiled as she looked at the leaf. "It's like the garden will always be with us, even when we're far away."

Before they could leave, Orin swooped down from a nearby branch and landed lightly beside them. "The lessons you've learned here—about patience, wisdom, and knowing when to act—will guide you. Remember, knowledge is always within reach when you slow down and listen."

Finn bounded up to Calvin, his tail wagging. "And don't forget the fun! Whatever challenge you face, there's always room for a little joy and adventure."

Seraphina approached gracefully, her mane shimmering in the morning light. "The magic of the garden lives within you now. Balance is delicate but strong. Keep that balance in your hearts, and it will serve you well in your world, just as it does here."

The garden's creatures—flowers, trees, and animals—gathered around Calvin and Krisa, offering their farewells. It wasn't a goodbye; it was a promise that the magic would always remain within them.

As Calvin and Krisa began their journey back to their own world, a soft glow appeared in the distance, much like the first time they arrived in the garden. It wasn't just the light of the garden—it was a reflection of the lessons and magic they had unlocked within themselves.

Calvin turned to Krisa; the leaf safely tucked into his pocket. "I think I'm ready for whatever comes next."

Krisa grinned back. "Me too. Whatever challenge we face, we'll remember the magic of the Enchanted Garden—and the lesson it taught us."

With that, they stepped forward, leaving the Enchanted Garden behind but knowing they would always carry its magic in their hearts. And now, Calvin had a piece of that magic—a small, glowing silver leaf—that he would take with him, a reminder of the world they had saved and the lessons they would never forget.

CHAPTER 8

A New World Awaits

Calvin nodded; his eyes wide with wonder. The air was cool and crisp, and the sky above them was painted in swirling shades of purple and blue. Stars twinkled in the distance, and far below, fluffy clouds drifted lazily by. In the distance, he saw floating islands, each one with towering castles made of shimmering crystal. Bridges made from rainbows stretched between the islands, and in mid-air, glowing gardens bloomed, their flowers whispering secrets to the wind.

"It's like a kingdom in the clouds," Calvin whispered in awe.

"It's called the Sky Kingdom," Krisa said with a smile. "A place where the rules of the world below don't apply. Anything can happen here."

...elegant dragons with scales that glittered like jewels in the starlight, sky whales whose songs were so deep they seemed to vibrate through the air, and playful cloud dolphins that leaped and spun through the sky, leaving trails of mist behind them.

The Next Adventure: THE SKY KINGDOM

To be continued…

Calvin's Dream Chronicles 3

The Sky Kingdom

CHAPTER 1

The Sky Kingdom Beckons

On another starry night, Calvin drifted into a dream, feeling the familiar pull of his imagination. This time, the dream felt different—brighter, bigger, and even more magical. As he floated higher and higher, he realized he was no longer on solid ground. He was soaring above the clouds in a mystical sky kingdom, a world so breathtaking it made him forget everything else.

Next to him, Krisa appeared, her glowing hair flowing like strands of golden light in the breeze. Her turquoise eyes sparkled with excitement as they looked out over the horizon. "Isn't this amazing?" she said softly, her voice carrying on the wind.

Calvin nodded, his eyes wide with wonder. The air was cool and crisp, and the sky above them was painted in swirling shades of purple and blue. Stars twinkled in the distance, and far below, fluffy clouds drifted lazily by. In the distance, he saw floating islands, each one with towering castles made of shimmering crystal.

Bridges made from rainbows stretched between the islands, and in mid-air, glowing gardens bloomed, their flowers whispering secrets to the wind.

"It's like a kingdom in the clouds," Calvin whispered in awe.

"It's called the Sky Kingdom," Krisa said with a smile. "A place where the rules of the world below don't apply. Anything can happen here."

As they floated through the magical realm, Calvin felt a rush of freedom. The world beneath them seemed so far away, and in this sky kingdom, he felt like he could do anything. Majestic creatures glided alongside them—elegant dragons with scales that glittered like jewels in the starlight, sky whales whose songs were so deep they seemed to vibrate through the air, and playful cloud dolphins that leaped and spun through the sky, leaving trails of mist behind them.

Krisa pointed toward a group of dragons soaring overhead, their wings stretching wide as they glided gracefully between the islands. "Look! They're heading to the Crystal Castle," she said. "Do you want to follow them?"

Calvin grinned, feeling a surge of excitement. "Definitely!"

The two friends soared higher, following the dragons as they glided effortlessly through the sky. The air seemed to hum with energy, and everywhere Calvin looked, there was something new and magical to discover. Rainbow-colored birds flew in flocks, their feathers shimmering in the light, while the floating islands below were filled with strange, glowing plants and creatures Calvin had never seen before.

But even in the beauty of the Sky Kingdom, Calvin could sense something else. Beneath the surface, there was a mystery waiting to be uncovered—something important they would need to discover if they were to truly explore the secrets of this magical world.

Krisa seemed to sense it too. "There's more to this place than meets the eye," she said thoughtfully. "The Sky Kingdom is full of wonder, but it also holds challenges. We'll have to be ready."

Calvin nodded, feeling his heart race with excitement and anticipation. The adventure had only just begun, and he couldn't wait to see what lay ahead in the Sky Kingdom.

Meeting Zephyr, the Sky Guardian

As I flew further into the Sky Kingdom, the dream felt more real with every passing moment. Krisa was right by my side, her colorful hair flowing behind her like a banner in the wind. We had left the floating islands and crystal castles behind for a moment, but now we found ourselves heading toward something even more magnificent.

We landed on a huge floating island, bigger than any I had seen before. It was covered in forests so green they looked like emeralds, and rivers of water sparkled as they twisted and turned in the air. Tall crystal towers rose up from the trees, and as the sun began to set, the whole island seemed to glow with rainbow colors that danced across the sky.

"Wow," I whispered, taking it all in. I wasn't sure if I was even breathing. Everything around me was too magical.

Krisa smiled at me, her eyes glowing with excitement. "I told you the Sky Kingdom was full of surprises!"

We started walking, and as soon as I stepped onto the island, I felt a cool breeze touch my skin. It smelled like fresh rain and blooming flowers, and the air itself seemed to shine with a soft, golden light. I didn't know it at the time, but that was when I first felt him—Zephyr, the Sky Guardian.

He appeared in front of us, like he had been part of the island the whole time. I'd never seen anyone like him. Zephyr was tall, with shimmering silver feathers that reflected the sunlight like a prism. His wings were folded at his sides, but I could see a faint glow coming from them, like they were filled with the light of the sky itself. His eyes—his eyes were the most incredible part. They were deep, swirling with blues and golds, like he had seen every sunrise and sunset there ever was.

"Welcome, Calvin. Welcome, Krisa," Zephyr said, his voice calm but powerful, like the rumble of distant thunder. "You have entered the Sky Kingdom, a place of wonder and adventure. I am Zephyr, the guardian of this realm."

I exchanged a glance with Krisa, who nodded. I could tell she felt the same sense of amazement that I did. Zephyr wasn't just some magical creature—he felt like part of the sky itself.

"It's beautiful here," I managed to say, still trying to take everything in. "What kind of adventures can we have in a place like this?"

Zephyr's eyes seemed to twinkle, and a small smile tugged at the corners of his mouth. "There are many secrets hidden among the clouds," he said. "But there is one treasure that has been lost for ages—the Celestial Crystal. It is a powerful gem that brings light and harmony to the Sky Kingdom. Without it, our world has grown dim, and the balance of this realm is in danger. Would you help me find it?"

The thought of a quest filled me with excitement. I had never been asked to do something so important. I looked at Krisa, and she smiled back at me, already knowing my answer. We couldn't pass this up.

"We'll help," I said, feeling a surge of energy. "What do we need to do?"

Zephyr's gaze softened, like he already knew we were the right ones for the job. "Our journey begins here," he said, spreading his wings wide. "Together, we will explore the skies and restore the light to the Sky Kingdom."

With that, Krisa and I followed Zephyr, ready for the adventure that awaited us. The sky above us was filled with wonders, and I knew that with Krisa by my side and Zephyr as our guide, we could face whatever challenges lay ahead.

CHAPTER 3

A Familiar Friend's Wisdom

As Zephyr and I stood at the edge of the floating island, the soft glow of the sky around us seemed to grow brighter, as if the Sky Kingdom itself was preparing for what lay ahead. Beside me, Krisa floated gracefully, her golden skin catching the light, her eyes glowing with excitement and curiosity. She had been with me since the start of this adventure, and her presence had made everything feel even more magical.

"Do you feel that?" Krisa asked, her voice filled with wonder as she gazed at the sky. "It's like the whole kingdom is alive, watching us."

I nodded. There was something special about this place—something that felt bigger than all of us. "Yeah, it's like it's waiting for us to do something important," I replied.

Zephyr spread his wings, the golden feathers shimmering softly in the light. "The Sky Kingdom is a living realm," he explained. "It responds to those who seek its secrets and are ready to protect its balance."

Krisa smiled thoughtfully, her colorful hair drifting gently in the breeze. "It reminds me of the underwater world," she said, her voice calm and warm. "There, everything was connected, like a delicate dance. I think it's the same here, but in the sky."

Her words made sense. Just like the underwater world, the Sky Kingdom felt like a place where everything was linked—every cloud, every creature, every floating island. Krisa had a way of seeing things, of understanding the magic that connected the worlds we traveled through, and it always amazed me.

Zephyr nodded in agreement. "Your insight is wise, Krisa. The Sky Kingdom thrives on balance, and that balance is fragile. The Celestial Crystal, which we seek, is the key to keeping that balance. Its light has kept this realm in harmony for centuries, but now that it's lost, our world is vulnerable."

The mention of the Celestial Crystal filled me with determination. This quest wasn't just about finding treasure—it was about restoring something vital to the kingdom. "We have to find it," I said, looking at Krisa and Zephyr. "Together, we can bring it back and protect this place."

Krisa's turquoise eyes met mine, her expression full of encouragement. "We've faced challenges before, Calvin, and we've always made it through. This time will be no different."

With Krisa's confidence and Zephyr's guidance, I felt ready for whatever lay ahead. The three of us stood together, a united team, prepared to face the mysteries and challenges of the Sky

Kingdom. With the sky glowing softly above us, we knew our journey was just beginning.

CHAPTER 4

The Quest for the Celestial Crystal

With the mission clear in our hearts, Krisa, Zephyr, and I set off on our journey through the Sky Kingdom. We glided from one floating island to the next, each one more incredible than the last. The sky above us shifted in colors—from deep blues to bright pinks and purples—like the sky itself was alive, changing with every moment. It felt like we were traveling through a dream, one woven from stars and clouds.

As we flew, we met all kinds of magical creatures. There were playful cloud sprites—tiny, see-through beings that floated in the breeze, leaving trails of sparkling mist behind them. Their laughter sounded like little bells, adding music to our adventure. High above, old silver eagles watched over the kingdom with sharp eyes that seemed to see everything. It was as if they could look right into our souls.

But the phoenixes were what really blew me away. These huge birds, with flames for feathers, streaked across the night sky, lighting up the darkness like shooting stars. Every time one cried out, it was like a song that echoed through the air, filled with hope and new beginnings. Krisa, Zephyr, and I listened closely as these creatures shared their stories—tales of the kingdom's past, its glories, and the challenges that had shaped it. Their wisdom helped guide us, giving us hints about the journey ahead.

Our first stop was the Isle of Echoes, a place unlike anything I had ever seen. Here, every sound was louder—every whisper, every footstep, even the wind itself. The island seemed to hum with life, as though it was singing a song we couldn't quite understand. As we stepped onto the island, a voice rose up around us. It didn't come from anyone we could see; it was like the island itself was speaking.

The voice asked us a riddle, its tone playful but mysterious. We huddled together, trying to figure it out. Krisa closed her eyes, thinking hard, while Zephyr listened to the wind for clues. The echoes around us seemed to help, bouncing our thoughts back to us until finally, we solved it. We had figured out the riddle! The reward was a beautiful crystal key, glowing with its own light—a reminder that when we work together, we're unstoppable.

From there, we journeyed to the Isle of Whispers. This island was quieter, but the air buzzed with secrets. As soon as we landed, I could hear soft whispers carried on the wind. They weren't loud, but they felt important—like the voices of ancient beings, long gone but not forgotten. The whispers told stories about the Sky Kingdom's history—about battles won and lost, about heroes who had lived and sacrificed for the kingdom.

Krisa closed her eyes, listening deeply, and Zephyr stood still, absorbing the whispers like they were a part of him. I let the whispers wash over me too, and as we listened, the past seemed to come alive. The whispers told us hidden truths and showed us paths we hadn't seen before, guiding us toward the Celestial Crystal.

Every step brought us closer to our goal. The Isle of Whispers taught us something important: that listening—truly listening—to each other, to the world around us, and to the wisdom of the past was the key to moving forward. Together, we felt stronger than ever, ready to face whatever challenges lay ahead as we continued our journey through the vast and magical Sky Kingdom.

CHAPTER 5

Trials of the Sky Kingdom

Our journey took us to the mysterious Isle of Stars, where the ground beneath our feet wasn't solid—it was made of shimmering clouds that seemed to glow with the light of distant stars. Every step felt like we were walking on a piece of the night sky, surrounded by constellations.

The maze in front of us wasn't like anything I'd ever seen before. The paths were made of clouds that twisted and shifted, disappearing and reappearing as we moved. One wrong step, and the ground beneath us could vanish, leaving us hanging in mid-air. It was both thrilling and terrifying.

"Stay focused," Krisa said, her voice steady as she took the lead. She seemed to understand the way the maze worked, sensing the patterns in the shifting paths. Her colorful hair flowed behind her as she moved gracefully, her turquoise eyes sharp with concentration. "We can do this. Just trust your instincts."

I took a deep breath, calming the nerves buzzing in my chest. Krisa's calm presence had always made me feel more confident, and here, in this strange maze, it was no different. I followed her lead, trusting her intuition and my own growing sense of the maze.

Zephyr, with his golden wings glowing softly, flew beside us, offering words of wisdom when the paths grew tricky. "Remember," he said, his voice calm but firm, "the maze is not just about finding your way. It's about working together, trusting each other."

The clouds beneath us twisted and shifted, sometimes vanishing altogether, but we didn't panic. With Krisa's sharp mind guiding us and Zephyr's calm advice keeping us focused, we moved as one. I found myself growing more confident with each step, relying on Krisa and Zephyr, but also trusting myself.

"Look ahead!" Krisa called, pointing toward a path that was starting to fade. Without hesitation, she darted forward, her movements graceful and sure. I followed, pushing past the fear of what could happen if the ground disappeared beneath me. With Krisa leading the way and Zephyr lighting our path, we made it through the maze, each step reminding me how much we had grown as a team.

When we finally reached the end of the maze, I felt a surge of pride. It hadn't been easy, but we had done it together. I glanced at Krisa, who smiled back at me, her eyes bright with the same sense of accomplishment I was feeling.

But our challenges weren't over yet. Next, we arrived at the Isle of Reflections. Unlike the dazzling Isle of Stars, this place was quiet, almost eerie. Pools of still water dotted the island, each one reflecting the sky above like a perfect mirror. But when I looked into the nearest pool, I didn't just see my reflection. I saw something deeper—my fears and doubts, the moments where I didn't believe in myself, and the worries I kept hidden.

A wave of unease washed over me, but Krisa was there, placing a comforting hand on my shoulder. "You're not alone, Calvin," she said gently, her voice filled with understanding. "We all have these fears."

Zephyr nodded in agreement. "These pools show us the truths we hide from ourselves," he said. "But facing those fears is the only way forward."

Krisa stepped up to one of the pools, gazing into the water with a calm, determined expression. "We've faced worse," she said quietly, as if speaking to her own reflection. "We can face this, too."

Her bravery gave me the strength to face my own fears. As we stared into the pools, riddles began to appear on the surface of the water, each one reflecting a part of ourselves we needed to confront. Krisa was the first to solve hers, her sharp mind cutting through the confusion. "It's not just about what we see," she said, her voice steady. "It's about what we believe in ourselves."

With Krisa's insight and Zephyr's wisdom, I found the courage to solve my riddle, too. Together, we pieced together the answers, each one revealing a new part of an ancient map. The pieces floated into the air, glowing softly before merging into a single, complete map.

The Isle of Reflections hadn't just tested our minds—it had tested our hearts. But with Krisa and Zephyr by my side, I knew we could handle whatever came next. As we left the island, I felt lighter, like a weight had been lifted from me. The path to the Celestial Crystal was clearer now, and with Krisa's unwavering support, I knew we were ready for whatever lay ahead.

CHAPTER 6

The Storm of Shadows

As we neared the final island, the sky around us began to change. The bright, beautiful colors faded, replaced by an unsettling darkness creeping in from every direction. The air felt heavy, like it was pressing down on us, and the soft breeze that had carried us so far turned into a harsh wind, howling like it had a mind of its own. Above us, dark clouds began to swirl, twisting and churning like they were alive, and I knew we were about to face something dangerous.

The Storm of Shadows had arrived.

My heart pounded in my chest as I watched the darkness grow. The shadows didn't just fill the sky—they formed into twisted, monstrous shapes, each one more terrifying than the last. Their glowing eyes stared at us with a cold, cruel light, and it felt like the once-beautiful Sky Kingdom had turned into a place of fear and danger.

A wave of terror hit me as the shadows closed in, their cold presence wrapping around us like a suffocating blanket. I could feel the fear creeping into my thoughts, whispering doubts and worries. What if we couldn't defeat the storm? What if we failed? But then, I looked at Zephyr, standing tall and strong, his golden wings glowing brightly, cutting through the darkness. Krisa stood beside him, her eyes shining with determination, her confidence as unshakable as ever.

"Stay close, Calvin," Zephyr said, his voice calm and steady. "These shadows feed on our fears and doubts. The more we let them take over, the stronger they become. But remember, the light within us can drive them away."

Zephyr's words stuck with me. I realized that these shadows weren't just monsters—they were born from our own fears, from the doubts we carried inside. If we wanted to banish them, we had to face those fears and find the light inside ourselves.

I took a deep breath, reaching out to hold Krisa's hand. She squeezed mine reassuringly, and I felt her strength flow into me. Together with Zephyr, we focused on the light in our hearts, letting it grow until it shone brightly. Zephyr's wings blazed like the sun, and Krisa's presence glowed softly beside me, filling the air with a warm, comforting light.

I closed my eyes, thinking about everything we had been through—the riddles, the challenges, and the strength we'd found in each other. I let that light fill me up, pushing back the fear that had crept into my mind.

As our combined light spread, the shadows began to shrink, their monstrous forms flickering and dissolving in the glow. The storm raged on, but with every pulse of light, the darkness was pushed back further. I could feel the struggle in the air, the clash between light and shadow growing more intense. My fear still lingered, but with Krisa and Zephyr by my side, I knew we could face it together.

The battle was fierce. The shadows kept coming, relentless in their attack, and for a moment, it felt like the darkness might overwhelm us. The storm roared louder, the wind howling in our ears, but we stood firm. Krisa's hand in mine, Zephyr's wings glowing bright, and my own heart filled with courage.

The shadows slowly began to weaken, their forms breaking apart into wisps of smoke that were carried away by the wind. The storm's power started to fade, the swirling black clouds parting to reveal patches of the sky's original beauty. The light we had created—our light—grew brighter and brighter, until it filled the entire sky, banishing the last of the shadows.

Finally, the storm was gone. The sky was clear again, the air calm and peaceful. A soft golden light illuminated the path ahead, leading us to the heart of the final island. I took a deep breath, feeling a wave of relief and accomplishment wash over me.

The Storm of Shadows had tested us in ways I hadn't expected, but we had faced our fears together and come out stronger. With Krisa and Zephyr beside me, I knew that no matter what challenges lay ahead, we would face them as a team, our light undimmed by the darkness.

78

Discovering the Celestial Crystal

As the last traces of the storm faded into harmless clouds, Krisa, Zephyr, and I found ourselves drawn to the heart of the island. Floating in the air before us, surrounded by a gentle swirl of mist and light, was the Celestial Crystal. It was breathtaking—a gem that glowed with brilliant colors, casting shimmering lights across the sky like a rainbow. The crystal pulsed with a steady rhythm, almost like the heartbeat of the Sky Kingdom itself.

I stared in awe. I had never seen anything so beautiful, so full of life and energy. The storm that had once surrounded us now felt like a distant memory, with only soft clouds remaining, peacefully drifting by. The air around us was calm and warm, like the whole kingdom was holding its breath, waiting for us to reach the crystal.

With a mixture of awe and excitement, I stepped forward. The light from the crystal seemed to reach out to me, filling me with a sense of peace I had never known before. Each step felt easier than the last, as if the crystal was pulling me closer, wrapping me in its warm glow. The fears and doubts I had faced in the storm melted away, replaced by a calm, steady feeling inside me.

When I finally reached out and touched the crystal, it felt like the entire Sky Kingdom came alive. A soft, gentle energy flowed through me—not overwhelming, but comforting. I could feel a connection with the kingdom around me, like the light inside the crystal was now a part of me too. It was as if I was linked to every floating island, every sky creature, and every star in the sky above.

In that moment, the last of the storm disappeared. The dark clouds that had once filled the sky were gone, replaced by soft, white puffs floating lazily in the bright blue sky. The floating islands, which had been covered in shadows, were now glowing with vibrant colors, more beautiful than I had ever seen them. The creatures of the sky—majestic dragons, playful cloud dolphins, and more—joined together in a joyful chorus, their songs filling the air with happiness.

Zephyr and Krisa stood beside me; their faces lit up by the crystal's glow. Zephyr's wise eyes sparkled with pride, and Krisa's smile was brighter than ever. Together, we stood in the crystal's light, celebrating the victory of our journey. We had done it. We had found the Celestial Crystal, and in doing so, we had restored balance to the Sky Kingdom.

But this moment wasn't just about finding the crystal. I realized that the Celestial Crystal wasn't just a treasure or a magical object—it was a symbol. It represented the courage, hope, and strength that had guided us through every challenge. The light inside the crystal was the same light we had found inside ourselves, the same light that had driven away the darkness.

As the crystal continued to shine its healing light across the kingdom, I felt a deep sense of joy and accomplishment. We had completed our quest, but more importantly, I had discovered something new about myself. The doubts and fears that had once held me back were gone, replaced by a confidence I hadn't known was inside me. I was stronger than I had ever realized.

The Sky Kingdom, now restored to its full beauty and harmony, was more magical than ever. As I stood there with my friends, surrounded by the glowing islands and the bright, open sky, I knew that this was just the beginning of many more adventures to come. The Celestial Crystal, with its endless light, would always remind me of the power of courage, hope, and the unbreakable bond of friendship.

CHAPTER 8

A New Beginning

As the light of the Celestial Crystal bathed the Sky Kingdom in a final, brilliant glow, I felt a warmth in my chest—a sense of accomplishment, but also something more. The sky had returned to its vibrant colors, the islands were full of life again, and everything felt... complete. I knew it was time to leave, but I also knew this wasn't the end.

Krisa stood beside me, her smile wide and bright. "You did it, Calvin," she said softly, her voice full of pride. "We did it."

I nodded, feeling a deep connection to her and to Zephyr. They had been with me through every challenge, and we had faced every fear together. The journey had changed me, and I knew I would carry this adventure with me forever.

As the dream world began to fade, Zephyr stepped forward, his golden wings shimmering in the soft light. He held something in his hands—a small, glowing feather, almost like a miniature version of his own wings. The feathers gleamed with a soft, radiant light that reminded me of the warmth and courage I had discovered here in the Sky Kingdom.

"Calvin," Zephyr said, his voice calm and wise, "I give you this feather, a piece of the Sky Kingdom's light. Keep it close to you, and whenever you feel doubt or fear, remember the strength you found here. The light of the Sky Kingdom will always be with you, just as the courage you found will guide you through every challenge ahead."

I reached out, carefully taking the glowing feather from Zephyr. It felt warm in my hand, radiating a quiet strength that filled me with peace. I smiled up at him, grateful beyond words.

"Thank you," I said, my voice full of emotion. "I'll never forget this place... or what I've learned here."

Zephyr bowed his head slightly, his eyes full of pride. "You have grown, Calvin. And this is only the beginning of your journey."

As the dream world continued to fade, the warmth of the Sky Kingdom and the glow of the feather stayed with me. This place—just like the underwater world and the magical forest—was a realm of endless possibilities. I knew that every night when I closed my eyes, I could return to these worlds, filled with new quests, new friends, and new wonders.

But more than that, I now carried a piece of the Sky Kingdom with me. The glowing feather was a reminder that even in the real world, when life felt uncertain, I had the courage and light inside me to face whatever came my way.

CHAPTER 9

Carrying the Light

The next morning, when I woke up, the feeling of the Sky Kingdom hadn't disappeared. The sunlight streaming through my window seemed a little brighter, and the world felt more alive. I smiled to myself, knowing that the magic of my dreams hadn't left me. It was still there, inside me.

Throughout the day, I thought about everything I had learned. There were challenges I faced in the real world too—problems at school, worries about fitting in, times when I felt uncertain. But now, whenever those moments came, I could close my eyes and remember the Celestial Crystal, glowing with the light of hope and courage. I could hear Krisa's encouraging words, see Zephyr's calm wisdom, and feel the strength that had helped me overcome every obstacle.

At school, when I was asked to give a presentation, I felt that familiar fear start to creep in. But instead of letting it take over, I thought of the Storm of Shadows and how we had defeated it. If I could face that, I could face anything. I took a deep breath, stood up in front of the class, and spoke with the same confidence I had found in the Sky Kingdom. And it worked.

That night, I couldn't wait to return to my dream worlds. As I closed my eyes, I knew that new adventures awaited me, but now I saw them differently. They weren't just stories—they were ways to learn, ways to grow, and ways to discover the best parts of myself.

CHAPTER 10

The Dream Continues

That night, I found myself standing on the edge of a new dream—a place I hadn't seen before. The sky was filled with stars, but there was something new in the air, something that promised adventure. Krisa appeared at my side, as she always did, her colorful hair sparkling in the starlight.

"Ready for the next journey?" she asked, her eyes twinkling with excitement.

I smiled. "Always."

And just like that, we were off, soaring into the unknown, ready for whatever challenges and wonders this new world had in store for us. I didn't know what lay ahead, but I wasn't afraid. I had learned that with courage, hope, and the power of friendship, anything was possible.

As we flew through the stars, I realized that my dreams would always be a part of me, guiding me in ways I hadn't understood before. Each dream was a new beginning, filled with endless possibilities. And with each adventure, I knew I would keep growing, learning, and finding the light within.

No matter where life took me, I would always have my dreams. And with them, I knew I could face anything.

The End (Or perhaps, the beginning of another adventure?)